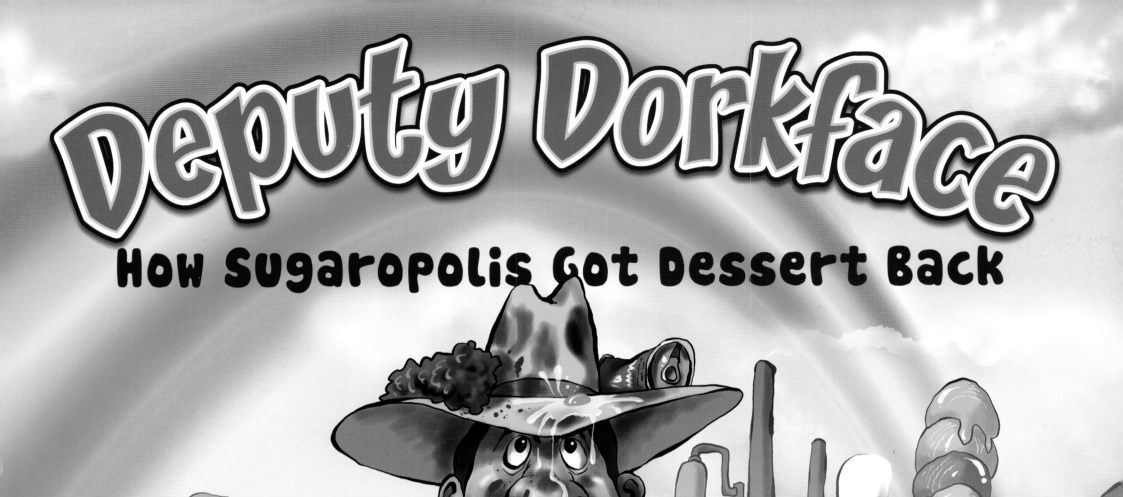

Art Direction: Sue Campbell
Illustration: Eldon Doty

Cataloging-in-Publication

Janison, Kevin.
  Deputy Dorkface : how Sugaropolis got dessert back /
Kevin Janison ; illustrated by Eldon Doty.
  32 p. : ill. ; 30 cm.

ISBN: 1-932173-98-6
ISBN-13: 978-1-932173-98-7

When Deputy Dorkface bans sweets of all kinds, the
children of Sugaropolis protest with a food fight, and then
negotiate a truce by agreeing to eat more wisely.

1. Diet—Adverse effects—Juvenile fiction. [1. Diet—Fiction.
2. Desserts—Fiction.] I. Title. II. Doty, Eldon, ill.

[E] dc22   2009   2008932927

Little League® is a registered trademark of Little League International.
Kisses® is a registered trademark of Hershey Company.

STEPHENS PRESS, LLC
A Stephens Media Company

Post Office Box 1600
Las Vegas, NV 89125-1600
www.stephenspress.com

Printed in Hong Kong

Dedicated to . . .

My wife Terri who makes sure we eat healthy
everyday. Her unwavering love keeps our
family happy and strong. Thank you!

MATTIE...
HAPPY READING!
-Kevin Janison

Deputy Dorkface

How Sugaropolis Got Dessert Back

Kevin D. Janison

Illustrated by Eldon Doty

Stephens Press • Las Vegas, Nevada

Once upon a time, in the western region of Sweetzerland, there was a dessert lovers paradise — Sugaropolis — the sweetest town on Earth.

Sugar cane grew in fields all around town. The bakery baked delicious pies, cakes, and pastries. The Donut Whole boasted thousands of whole donuts and donut holes! And the 10,031 Flavors advertised that many kinds of ice cream.

The overwhelming and tantalizing aroma of yummy sweets drifted from every direction.

Yummmmmm-meeee.

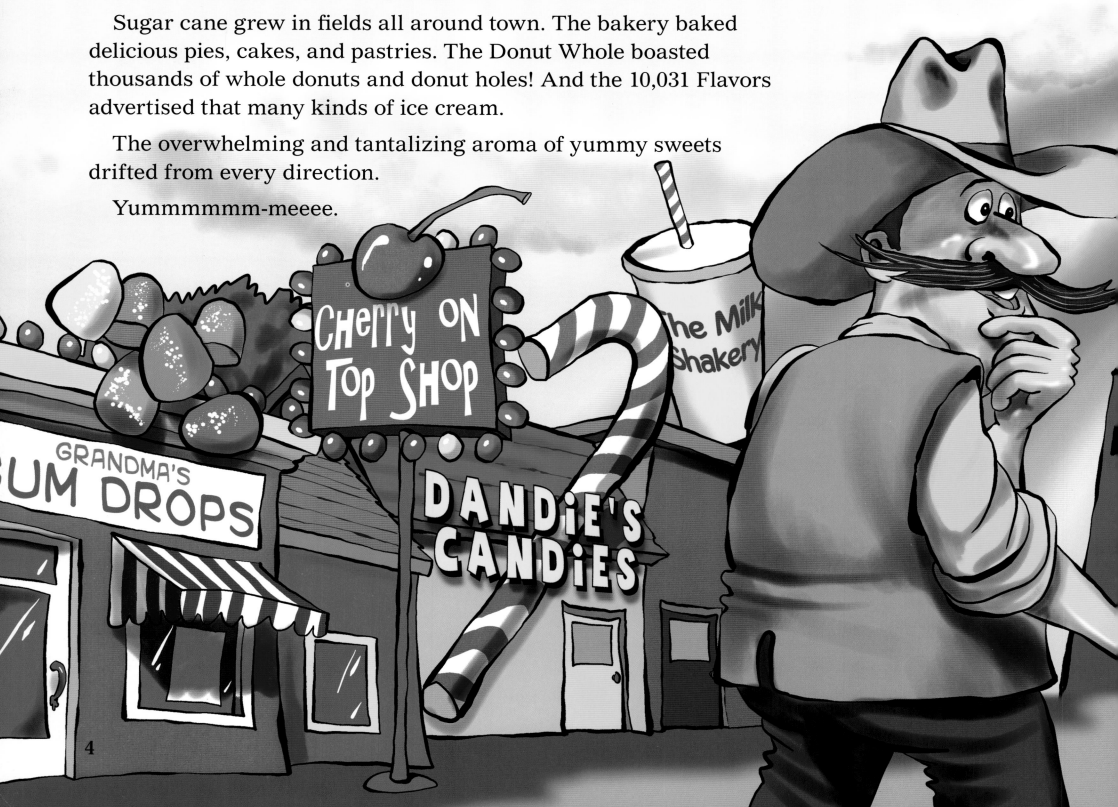

At the Dessert First Diner, guests could spin the "Wheel of Frosting" before *AND* after dinner to win a free dessert. The wheel was filled with pictures of pies, ice cream sundaes, cookies, cakes, and shakes. Lucky diners waited eagerly for the arrow to point to the sweet additions to their meal!

6

On Candy Cane Lane, Carly and Hailey enjoyed a freshly made chocolate cream pie. Over on Rocky Road, Andrew and Kyle stuck their fingers into the vanilla icing on the marble cake Kyle's mom had baked.

Yummmmmm-meeee.

In Sugaropolis, dessert was special. For years, everyone, especially kids, couldn't wait to get past the meatloaf and green peas to gobble up sweets of every kind.

Life for the sugary town's residents was extremely tasty until strange things began to occur all around the community.

Last Saturday, a Little League player, running from second to third, dropped in his tracks and sprawled out for a snooze.

Over on the school playground, kids were playing hopscotch. Mysteriously, their teeth dropped right out of their mouths.

The 100-yard dash turned into a stroll that lasted 30 minutes.

The annual Sugaropolis Swimming Pool Cannonball Competition produced a flash flood.

8

At the high school dance, the two-step was reduced to one. School had to be extended to 6:30 p.m., because the students needed a nap to get through the day.

Finally, parents reported a shocking discovery. The kids didn't have enough energy to play video games — their thumbs were too tired!

One evening, Dylan Dorkface, son of Deputy Dorkface, told Mama Dorkface that he was just too full to finish his dinner. However, just minutes later, Dylan asked his mom, "What's for dessert?"

Too full for dinner, but plenty of room for dessert?

What's going on here? thought Deputy Dorkface. As the town's only official, the deputy knew he had to do SOMETHING! So, he jammed his deputy hat on his head, not quite straight, and raced out the door.

As always, most Sugaropolians were glued to the Chocolate Channel on Sweetzerland Cable TV. Suddenly, the volume lowered, followed by three long, loud beeps.

BEEEEEP, BEEEEEP, BEEEEEP.

The deputy's face filled the screen. He cleared his throat and proceeded with a special announcement:

SCTV BAN INCLUDES: CAKES, CANDY, ICE CREAM, SHAKES... 6:02 PM
CARROTS▲ COCOA▼ CORN SYRUP▼ SPINACH▲ SUGAR▼ LIVE

"This is Deputy Dorkface here with an emergency bulletin for the health, safety, and well-being of all Sugaropolians. It has come to my attention that the young people of Sugaropolis are not behaving like regular kids. The reason is too many sweets! So, to return Sugaropolis to the city it once was, I officially proclaim: Hereto, whereunder, thereby, from this day forthwith, all desserts, candy, sodas, cookies, ice cream, shakes, and cakes are BANNED! We now continue with our regularly scheduled programming."

Uh Oh! No more . . .

Yummmmmm-meeee.

Moans and groans erupted from homes all over the city. Kids ran to the kitchen for their last bites of sweet treats before the Dessert Police came by to collect the goodies. Residents caught concealing candy, cakes, and other assorted desserts were sentenced to one year of eating only cauliflower and eggplant with mustard. Yuck!

Beans hurt our spleens.

Chores for S'mores

Send my Veggies to Venus!

Cookies NOT Cabbage!

Shocked and upset kids ran outside into the streets. By 8 p.m., a mob of young Sugaropolians arrived at their secret clubhouse in the trees of Peppermint Park. The kids' shouts and loud exclamations drowned out Hailey who tried to call the meeting to order.

"This is not fair!"

"I'm never going to eat again!"

"Cauliflower with mustard? Ick!"

"My mom put my birthday candles on liver!"

"Oh yeah, well after dinner I got frozen pig knuckles!"

"I don't want to eat a bunch of vegetation!"

"All we have are beans: baked, green, black, pinto, lima, soy, and refried."

Hailey banged the gavel and yelled above the clamor, "This emergency meeting of the Kids of Sugaropolis must come to order! Calm down! We need ideas to get our dessert back!"

"Yeah . . . absolutely . . . oh yes, please!" shouted the young, overflow crowd packed into the treehouse.

The super-secret gathering lasted more than an hour. When the kids left the meeting, they wore determined faces. They all wanted to seize their desserts back right now.

Outside of the clubhouse, Carly nailed their declaration to the tree. It was signed by all of the kids and it said this:

We can't live without sweets.
We want our desserts.
You can't do this to us.
We, the Kids
of Sugaropolis
DECLARE WAR!
We declare a
FOOD FIGHT!
You have been warned.

Taylor   Stacey   Terri
Carly   Carolyn   Colin
Andrew   Hailey   Kyle   Suzanne   José
Dylan   Eldon
Kevin   Krissy   Serena   Maria   Brownie

When the sun rose the very next morning, the day seemed quiet, peaceful, and normal. But, when the last school bell rang, something was very different.

First, the students achieved their highest scores on their math tests. Then the kids ran home from school with more energy than before. It was energy that the kids soon put to a mischievous use.

While Deputy Dorkface was out on patrol, his vehicle was abruptly t-boned by a t-bone. He jumped out of his car to find the culprits and another group of kids peppered him with pepper. Sneezing and snorting, Deputy Dorkface screamed, "I'll get you kids! I'll throw you all in the slammer!"

The deputy rushed to his car to call his fellow officers. Then the kids stretched bubble gum around the car. He was stuck! When the Sugaropolis police cruisers arrived, they couldn't avoid the falling and exploding watermelons being launched from the roof of a nearby building.

One policeman slammed on his brakes so hard that the airbags deployed. But the kids had filled the airbags with marshmallow cream and a sticky, sugary mess exploded all over the officer. He could hardly move and everything he touched stuck to him!

The food fight lasted for two hours. Even Dylan Dorkface joined the melée. He loaded the fire hydrant with chocolate syrup and sprayed his dad until he resembled a giant hot fudge sundae. The deputy was not amused.

24

Some kids used slingshots to catapult tomatoes at Deputy Dorkface. Others used licorice and candy canes for bows and arrows.

The fracas turned into a complete mess. The National Guard came in helicopters! The kids were surrounded and trapped, and now they were in big, BIG trouble.

25

The perpetrators of the biggest, gooiest mess Sugaropolis had ever seen were rounded up in the town square. One by sticky one, the kids were loaded into a huge paddy wagon and taken to the police station.

Deputy Dorkface let the kids sit in jail for a while to think about what they had done. At the same time, a large group of concerned parents gathered outside. The moms and dads were really angry. The kids knew that while they were in trouble now — that was nothing compared to the big, BIG trouble they had coming once they were released — IF they were released.

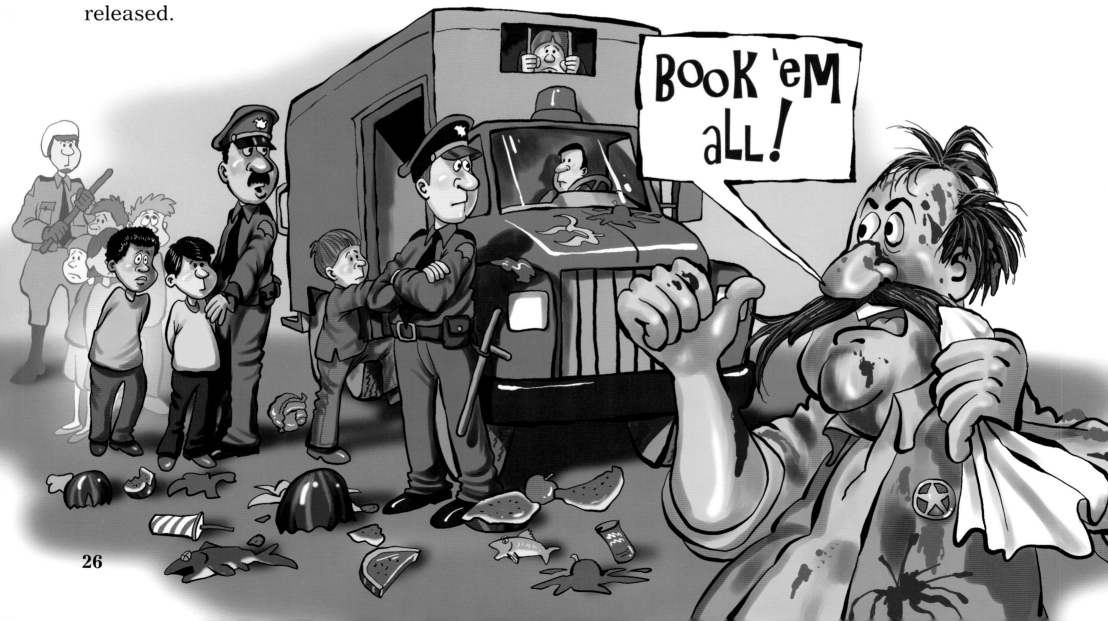

BOOK 'EM aLL!

After what felt like a really long time behind bars (it was only 15 minutes), several kids asked if they could speak with Deputy Dorkface.

The Deputy was wiping off the food that had been thrown his way. He still had sticky caramel in his hair, and he asked, "Why should I listen to you?"

"Because I have an idea," announced an embarrassed Carly, who had pelted a peace officer with chocolate kisses.

27

It got very quiet in the station as each of the kids apologized and proposed their ideas to the deputy. They hoped Sugaropolis would return to the sweet, but healthy city it had been before Deputy Dorkface had to ban dessert.

Kyle offered, "What happens if we promise to eat more salad?" Then other kids piped up with their own suggestions.

Deputy Dorkface just listened. After a while, he asked, "Just salad? What about a pound of asparagus for each of you every day?"

"No way! How about two carrots?" Andrew countered.

"Two carrots? Are you crazy? It'll have to be six avocados, three artichokes, an onion, and a zucchini. Each day!" the deputy shot back.

Inside the station, intense negotiations commenced. The kids and Deputy Dorkface listened to each other's demands, but it was up to the kids to offer something convincing. After all, they were the ones in jail!

Finally after six hours of talking, a breakthrough!

It was well past midnight when Deputy Dorkface and the kids walked out of the building together with an agreement. On the steps of city hall, they announced to all the gathered parents, and to the Chocolate Channel TV cameras that were broadcasting the announcement live:

"We, the kids of Sugaropolis, hereby agree to eat 75 percent of our dinner, which includes 80 percent of our vegetables and 50 percent of any additional side dish before we are eligible for dessert. We will exercise and play outdoors more. We also agree to help clean up after dinner. Also, we will. . . .

Just then, Carly jabbed Hailey in the ribs with her elbow and whispered loud enough for all to hear, "Enough already!"

30

The crowd of onlookers and kids cheered. The excited children raced into the arms of their weary parents.

Moms and dads were happy to have their children back, but the kids were still grounded for their part in the food fight.

From that day on, families of Sugaropolis exercised and played together. And sweets tasted even sweeter when they followed a healthy meal.

The day the kids stopped being grounded, they brought a special treat to Deputy Dorkface. "What's this?" the deputy asked suspiciously. "I can't eat sweets before my dinner!"

"But Dad," exclaimed Dylan Dorkface, "It's carrot cake!"

Eveyone enjoyed a laugh, and Sugaropolis, Sweetzerland was the sweetest town once again. Yummmmmm-meeee.